For David

First published 2002 by Walker Books Ltd
87 Vauxhall Walk, London SE11 5HJ

This edition published 2003

2 4 6 8 10 9 7 5 3 1

© 2002 Anita Jeram

The right of Anita Jeram to be identified as author/illustrator of this work
has been asserted by her in accordance with the Copyright, Designs and Patents Act 1988

This book has been typeset in Cochin

Printed in China

British Library Cataloguing in Publication Data:
a catalogue record for this book is available from the British Library

ISBN 978-0-7445-9462-1

www.walker.co.uk

I Love My Little Story Book

Anita Jeram

I love my little story book.

I love the way it looks.

I love the way it feels.

I love the places

I can go to in my

story book.

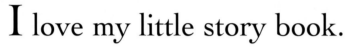

There's a magic forest
in my story book
where all my favourite flowers
and ferns and mushrooms grow.
My special friends are there.
I say hello.

There's a lion
in the magic forest.
Of course he is a very
friendly lion.

I go into my story book

and come out of it

whenever I like.

It shades me on a sunny day.

I love to make its pages flick

so I can feel the breeze.

There are fairies
in the magic forest
in my story book.

And there's a magic lake

for swimming in.

I dive deep down where

the underwater creatures live.

I go where I like

in my story book.

I can jump over my story book
if I want to.

I can wriggle under it.

My story book is full of
adventures and surprises.

There's a giant in the magic forest

in my story book.

When he comes stomping by,

I hide so he cannot see me.

In the heart of the magic forest there's a palace where Beauty lies asleep.

She stays asleep
until a prince finds her
and kisses her.

I love my little story book.

It makes my wishes come true.

The prince came and

kissed Beauty …

and there was a party
in the magic forest.

It was the best party ever.
Even the gentle lion
and the giant came.

When I'm tired I say goodbye

to my special friends before

I close my story book.

I love my little story book.

It makes me very happy.

I love it from the beginning

all the way

right through to …

the end

Also illustrated by Anita Jeram

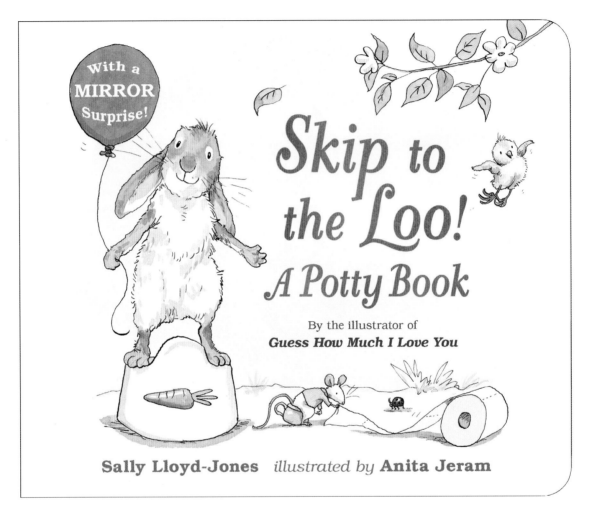

With a **MIRROR** Surprise!

Skip to the Loo! A Potty Book

By the illustrator of **Guess How Much I Love You**

Sally Lloyd-Jones illustrated by **Anita Jeram**

ISBN 978-1-4063-7734-7

Available from all good booksellers

www.walker.co.uk